To prevent color transfer to other pages, please place an extra sheet of paper between the pages before coloring.

THE FOOL

Meet the adorable Fool, ready to embark on a magical adventure! With a carefree spirit and a joyful heart, this little cutie is all about new beginnings and endless possibilities.

THE FOOL

THE MAGICIAN

Say hello to the charming Magician, a true master of magic! With a twinkle in their eye and a wand in hand, they're here to remind you that you have all the power you need to create your destiny.

THE MAGICIAN

THE HIGH PRIESTESS

Meet the sweet and mysterious High Priestess, the keeper of secrets and intuition. She sits with her kitty, sharing whispers of wisdom and guiding you to trust your inner voice.

THE HIGH PRIESTESS

THE EMPRESS

The lovely Empress is surrounded by flowers and nature, radiating warmth and love. She's all about creativity, nurturing, and embracing the beauty of life.

THE EMPRESS

THE EMPEROR

The cute and strong Emperor stands tall, offering protection and guidance. With a crown on his head and a heart whole of courage, he represents stability and leadership.

THE EMPEROR

THE HIEROPHANT

This adorable Hierophant is all about learning and tradition. With books around and a smile, they're here to teach you the joy of wisdom and spirituality.

THE HIEROPHANT

THE LOVERS

Meet the sweet Lovers, a duo of pure love and harmony. Holding hands and surrounded by hearts, they remind you of the magic of connection and relationships.

THE LOVERS

THE CHARIOT

The determined Chariot is ready to race forward with confidence! With a bright smile and trusty steed, this card represents victory, willpower, and determination.

THE CHARIOT

STRENGTH

The gentle Strength card features a sweet character with a lion friend, showing the power of kindness and inner courage. Together, they remind you that true strength comes from within.

STRENGTH

THE HERMIT

Holding a lantern, the wise Hermit is on a cozy quest for inner peace. Wrapped in a warm cloak, this card invites you to take some quiet time for reflection and self-discovery.

THE HERMIT

#10

WHEEL OF FORTUNE

The playful Wheel of Fortune spins with excitement and surprise! Covered in stars and good luck charms, it shows that life is full of ups and downs, but every turn brings new opportunities.

WHEEL OF FORTUNE

#11

JUSTICE

The fair and balanced Justice card holds scales and a sword, promoting harmony and truth. It reminds us that fairness and integrity are always in style.

JUSTICE

#12

THE HANGED MAN

The cheerful Hanged Man hangs upside down with a smile, seeing the world from a different angle. This card is all about gaining new perspectives and embracing change.

THE HANGED MAN

#13

DEATH

The cute and spooky Death card isn't scary at all! With a friendly skeleton and blooming flowers, it represents transformation and the start of something new.

DEATH

TEMPERANCE

The serene Temperance card mixes water with grace, symbolizing balance and harmony. With a peaceful aura, it encourages patience and moderation.

TEMPERANCE

#15

THE DEVIL

The mischievous Devil card features a playful character with tiny horns and a cheeky grin. It's a fun reminder to be aware of temptations and to stay true to yourself.

THE DEVIL

#16

THE TOWER

The dramatic Tower card shows a cute building struck by lightning, with stars and sparks flying around. It symbolizes sudden change and the excitement of new beginnings.

THE TOWER

#17

THE STAR

The enchanting Star card sparkles with hope and inspiration. Surrounded by twinkling stars, this card encourages you to dream big and believe in your magic.

THE STAR

#18

THE MOON

The dreamy Moon card glows with mystery and imagination. With a crescent moon and cute little critters, it invites you to explore your dreams and intuition.

THE MOON

#19

THE SUN

The joyful Sun card shines bright with happiness and positivity. With a big smiling sun and cheerful stars, it's all about warmth, success, and fun!

THE SUN

#20

JUDGMENT

The lively Judgment card features cute angels playing trumpets, calling for renewal and transformation. It's a fun reminder to embrace new beginnings and trust your inner calling.

JUDGEMENT

#21

THE WORLD

The cheerful World card dances in a circle of happiness and fulfillment. Surrounded by stars and sparkles, it celebrates completion, achievement, and the joy of wholeness.

THE WORLD

★ ★ ★ ★ ★

If you enjoyed this book, please leave us a review.

 LILOOT

Check out our website for more services:

Spiritual and Psychic Readings

Spiritual Guides

Personalized Candles & more

LILOOT.COM

Made in the USA
Columbia, SC
23 October 2024

44912886R00030